PUPPY PLACE

Scout

ELLEN MILES

SCHOLASTIC

For Chica Maria and her girls, Zoe and Luna

First published in the US by Scholastic Inc., 2007
This edition published in the UK by Scholastic Ltd, 2008
Scholastic Children's Books
An imprint of Scholastic Ltd
Euston House, 24 Eversholt Street
London, NW1 1DB, UK
Registered office: Westfield Road, Southam, Warwickshire, CV47 0RA
SCHOLASTIC and associated logos are trademarks and or registered trademarks of
Scholastic Inc.

Text copyright © Ellen Miles, 2007

The right of Ellen Miles to be identified as the author of this work
has been asserted by her.

10 digit ISBN 1 407 10601 5
13 digit ISBN 978 1407 10601 4

British Library Cataloguing-in-Publication Data.
A CIP catalogue record for this book is available from the British Library

Printed in the UK by CPI Bookmarque Ltd, Croydon,CR0 4TD
Papers used by Scholastic Children's Books are made from wood grown in
sustainable forests.

7 9 10 8 6

www.scholastic.co.uk/zone

Chapter One

"Let's see, are we about to miss the exit for the airport?" Meg squinted at a sign. "No, there we are. It's coming right up."

"I can't wait to get there!" Lizzie bounced in her seat. She could hardly believe that Meg had invited her along on this trip. They were going to pick up a very special puppy.

Meg Parker, who was on the Littleton fire squad with Lizzie's dad, was one of Lizzie Peterson's favourite people. Meg was a "dog person", just like Lizzie. They both loved dogs and everything about them.

"Tell me again," Lizzie asked Meg. "Tell me everything you know about this puppy."

"Well, she was born on a farm in Ohio, and her

1

name is Scout," Meg said. "She's named after a character in one of my favourite books, *To Kill a Mockingbird*."

"Scout," Lizzie repeated. She'd never read the book, but she liked the name. It was perfect for a young German shepherd puppy. "And you said she's four months old?"

"That's right," said Meg. "She's the same age Casey was when I rescued her."

Casey was Meg's five-year-old German shepherd. Casey had been abandoned as a puppy, and Meg had given her a home. That's what Meg meant by "rescued". Lizzie knew that there were lots and lots of puppies and dogs that needed homes. Meg loved German shepherds, and she liked to help them find perfect homes. Sometimes that meant working with other German shepherd lovers all over the country. Meg's German shepherd rescue group passed the word whenever a dog or puppy needed a home. Today, Meg had invited Lizzie to come with her to pick up Scout, who was arriving by airplane all the way from Ohio!

Meg knew of three different families who were hoping to give a German shepherd puppy a home. That's why Lizzie and Meg were zipping along the motorway in Meg's bright blue van. The van had a special area in the back for Casey, with a box called a crate where she could be safe. Meg had left Casey at Lizzie's house so the new puppy, Scout, could ride in the van today.

Meg and Casey travelled in the bright blue van a lot, because Casey was a search-and-rescue dog. Meg had trained Casey for years, and now they worked together as a team. "Maybe it's because she was rescued herself," Meg had told Lizzie, "but she really seems to love rescuing others."

Lizzie knew that search-and-rescue dogs and their owners went everywhere they were needed. They went to national parks if a child was lost in the woods. They also went to places where there had been earthquakes and people needed help, and to snowy areas where skiers got trapped by avalanches. Dogs like Casey were trained to use their sense of smell to track down people, no matter how lost they were. Working with Meg, Casey had saved the lives of many people. She was a hero.

Casey was clever and beautiful, and she was one of Lizzie's favourite dogs. Lizzie had *lots* of favourite dogs. In fact, she loved pretty much every dog she met. But certain dogs were special. Like Casey. And like Buddy, the puppy that Lizzie's family had adopted not long ago.

Buddy was one of the many puppies that the Petersons had fostered. Being a foster family meant that they took care of puppies who needed homes, just until the perfect for ever families came along. Lizzie and her younger brother Jack had convinced their parents that fostering puppies was a great family activity. The Bean, their toddler brother (whose real name was Adam), did not need any convincing. He *loved* puppies – in fact, he seemed to think he *was* one. He loved to pretend he was a dog. Sometimes Lizzie thought that the Bean believed Buddy was his little brother instead of a puppy!

Buddy was tan, with some brown markings and a white heart-shaped mark on his chest. He had been a tiny puppy, the runt of his litter. (That meant he was smaller than his two sisters.) But by now he had grown into a happy, healthy puppy. He was the sweetest guy! Lizzie loved to cuddle with him after a long play session. He would lick her face, snuggle into her lap, and fall asleep. His soft, warm puppy fur smelled so good. Lizzie felt like she could kiss his silky ears and pat his round pink belly all day long. She loved that little puppy so much.

Sometimes, Lizzie still could not believe that her parents had agreed to adopt Buddy. She and Jack had wanted a dog of their own for so long! Every time they had fostered a puppy, they had hoped to keep it. But it was never quite the right time

5

for the Petersons to adopt a dog. Instead, they found each puppy the perfect home. Then Buddy came along, and everybody in the family fell in love with him. Now he was theirs for ever.

Lizzie felt so lucky to have a dog to love. And she knew Buddy was lucky, too, to have found a loving family like hers. She wanted every puppy to find the right home.

"How will you decide which family gets to adopt Scout?" Lizzie asked Meg as they turned into the airport parking lot.

"Well, the Goodmans have been waiting the longest," Meg said. "So I'll probably call them first. I'll do that as soon as we make sure that Scout is healthy and that all her papers are in order." She pulled the van into a parking spot. "Ready?" she asked Lizzie. "Let's go meet Scout. I think that plane that's just about to land is probably hers." Meg pointed to a small white plane with red markings that was circling the airport.

Lizzie watched as the plane swooped down and

bumped onto the runway. It rolled along until it stopped near the airport terminal.

The plane's pilot belonged to a group called Wings of Love, whose members were dedicated to helping animals. Lizzie had heard about them before, but this was the first time she had seen them in action. She watched with excitement as the plane's door opened.

A tall man jumped out and waved to Meg. "Got your dog!" he called. "She's a sweetheart, too." He ducked back into the plane and came out a moment later, holding a little brown-and-black puppy in his arms.

The puppy looked up at the sky and blinked. Then she yawned, stretching out one small paw.

"Aw, what a cutie!" said Meg.

"Ohh!" Lizzie loved the puppy right away.

Scout had arrived.

Chapter Two

"Lizzie, do you want to hold Scout while we go over her paperwork?" Meg asked.

Lizzie's eyes were shining. Did she want to hold Scout? Oh, yes, she did. She could hardly wait. In a moment, the puppy was in her arms. Lizzie buried her nose in Scout's soft fur. "Welcome to Littleton, Scout!" she murmured.

Scout felt warm and safe in the girl's arms. The airplane ride had been fun but a little bit loud and scary. Scout loved adventure, but she also loved hugs.

"Here's her rabies certificate and the rest of her medical history," the pilot was saying. He handed some papers to Meg. "She's a very healthy little girl, and she's up to date on all her shots."

Meg was nodding, but Lizzie wasn't really listening. She was looking down at the puppy in her arms.

Scout was absolutely adorable. Her coat was fluffy and soft, and her eyes were the deepest, darkest brown. Her ears, which looked almost too big for her body, were flopped over in the cutest way. Lizzie knew that German shepherd puppies started out with floppy ears. As Scout got older, her ears would stand up straight, and she would look more like the German shepherds in books and films.

Lizzie knew some people were afraid of German shepherds. She wasn't sure why. Maybe it was because some of them were trained to be guard dogs, so they were supposed to look and act scary.

Meg's dog, Casey, was the sweetest, gentlest dog in the world. Even Lizzie's mum, who could sometimes be nervous around big dogs, loved Casey and trusted her around the Bean.

Lizzie knew that not all dogs were good with toddlers, but Casey was always very patient, even if the Bean put his fingers in her ears. Casey got along well with Buddy, too. The two dogs loved keeping each other company.

As for Scout, how could *anyone* be afraid of a puppy this cute? Lizzie nuzzled the puppy's neck again as Meg finished up with the pilot. Then she helped Meg put Scout into the crate in the back of the van. "I wish she could just stay on my lap," Lizzie said.

"I know, but she'll be safer back there." Meg checked the rearview mirror. "She's already sleeping, anyway!"

Lizzie turned back to see. Sure enough, Scout was curled up in a tiny, furry ball, with her head resting on one of Casey's stuffed toys. "Aww." What an adorable puppy.

On the way home, Meg told Lizzie stories about some of the amazing things Casey had done as a search-and-rescue dog. "You should see her when she's working," Meg said. "She's all business. I couldn't distract her even if I waved a hot dog in front of her face."

"I'd *love* to see her track somebody," Lizzie said.

Meg grinned. "Well, you're in luck," she said. "It just so happens that Casey and I are doing a demonstration at your school this Friday. My friend James, who's a policeman with a K-9 partner, is coming, too."

"Really? Cool!" That was definitely something to look forward to.

When they pulled into the Petersons' driveway, Jack and the Bean ran out to meet them. "Where's the puppy?" Jack asked. He peeked into the van's rear window. "Oh, she's so cute!" He boosted the Bean up so he could see, too.

"Uppy!" shouted the Bean.

"Do you think Scout will get along with Casey and Buddy?" Lizzie asked Meg.

"Let's find out," Meg said. "Maybe we can introduce them in the backyard, where they'll have room to run around."

"I'll let Buddy and Casey out!" Jack said. He headed back inside while Lizzie helped Meg get Scout out of the van.

The Bean laughed his googly laugh when he saw Scout in Lizzie's arms. He held up his hands. "Uppy! Uppy! Uppy!"

"He wants to hug her," Lizzie told Meg. "Maybe later," she said to her little brother. But she let him pat Scout, and she watched carefully to see what Scout thought of the Bean.

Scout liked the way the little boy patted her. He was gentle, even though his voice was loud. She had a feeling he was going to be a good friend.

Lizzie's mum and dad came out on to the deck facing the back garden to watch the dogs meet one another. "Oh, what a sweetie!" said Mum.

"She looks a lot like Casey when Casey was young," Dad said. "If she turns out half as good as Casey, she'll be a great dog." Casey spent a lot of time at the fire station, and Lizzie knew all the firefighters loved her.

Buddy and Casey had trotted over to find out what everyone was so interested in. When Casey saw Scout, her ears pricked up and she started to whine with excitement. Buddy was excited, too. He put his paws up on Lizzie and tried to reach his shiny black button nose up to touch Scout's.

Oh, boy! A new friend! Buddy liked Casey, but she was kind of boring. She didn't want to run and tumble and play. This smaller dog might be much more fun!

Scout did not seem shy at all. She wriggled in Lizzie's arms as if she wanted to get down and play. "What do you think?" Lizzie asked Meg.

"I think they'll be fine," Meg answered. "Go ahead and put her down."

The minute Lizzie put Scout down, she and the other two dogs began to sniff one another. Their tails were wagging hard. Scout nibbled on Casey's chin, and Casey put a soft paw on her as if to say, "Hey there, little one!" Buddy jumped around Scout, bowing with both front paws out in front of him. Lizzie knew what *he* was saying: *"Let's play! Let's play!"*

Then the two puppies took off, zooming around the yard as fast as their little legs could carry them. They tumbled and somersaulted and nipped and growled little puppy play growls. Casey trotted after them like a worried mother hen.

"Buddy has found a pal!" Lizzie said.

"And Casey has found a baby to care for," Meg added. "I think Scout's in good hands." She pulled out her mobile phone. "Now, to tell the Goodmans the good news!" She punched in a number and stepped aside to call Scout's new family.

Chapter Three

"Hello?" Lizzie heard Meg say. "Mrs Goodman?"

Lizzie knew that it was a very good thing that Scout had a wonderful home just waiting for her. Still, she couldn't help feeling a little bit sad that she would have to say goodbye to this very special puppy so soon.

But Lizzie couldn't stay sad for long. Just then Buddy ran past her, dragging a rope tug toy that was almost bigger than he was. Scout galloped behind him, trying to catch up with Buddy – and also trying to bite the other end of the rope. Doing two things at once was a bit too much for the little pup, and Lizzie laughed as Scout tumbled over her own feet. Casey brought up the rear, looking like the mature and dignified dog she was. That is, until she grabbed the toy and swung it away, teasing the younger pups by stealing their prize.

Lizzie and Jack and their parents could not stop laughing as they watched the three dogs playing. It was quite a sight. Scout was the smallest. She looked like a miniature Casey, only fluffier and with those flopped-over ears. Buddy was bigger, about up to Casey's shoulder. He had grown since the Petersons had adopted him, but he was still a roly-poly puppy who liked to chase his tail and still sometimes – not often, but sometimes! – made messes in the house.

And Casey? She was such a beautiful dog. Lizzie loved her alert, sharp-nosed face and her huge, soft brown eyes. Her coat was thick and shiny, a mix of brown, tan, and black. When Casey stood still with her head held high, she looked noble and elegant, like a hero. But then she would wag her long, feathery tail, give a doggy grin, and beg for a treat like any normal dog.

Right now, Casey was trotting along the fence

with the rope toy in her mouth. Both puppies were tearing after her. "She's playing keep-away!" Jack pointed and laughed. "She won't let them get the toy, no matter how hard they try!"

Lizzie was laughing, too. But then she saw Casey lurch and stumble. When she regained her balance and started to walk again, she was limping a little. "Oh, no!" Lizzie ran over to Casey. "Are you OK?" She put her arms around the dog.

"She's fine," Meg said, snapping her mobile phone shut and coming over to join Lizzie. She felt Casey's front leg. "You're OK, sweetie, right?" She turned to Lizzie. "She just has an old shoulder injury that acts up sometimes. It's no big deal."

"So, are you taking Scout to the Goodmans?" Lizzie bit her lip.

"Well," Meg said. "Actually, I'm not. It turns out they can't take her. Mrs Goodman just had a bad fall and broken her leg, and she's going to be on crutches for quite a while. It's just not a good time for them to have a puppy." She sighed. "Oh, well. I'll call the Tanakas. They were second on my list." She opened up her phone again, and Lizzie turned back to watch the dogs.

"Check out Buddy!" Jack said. "He really likes Scout. See how he's chewing on her ear?"

"I think Buddy likes being a big brother," Lizzie agreed. "And look at Casey. She *loves* Scout. They could almost be mother and daughter." Lizzie looked up at her mum. "They're not scary at all, right?"

"Not a bit," said Mum. "Anyway, Meg tells me that German shepherds are rarely mean dogs, unless someone trains them to be nasty."

"That's right," said Meg, snapping her phone shut again. "Most German shepherds are total pussycats."

"So?" Lizzie asked. "Are the Tanakas excited about their new puppy?"

Meg rolled her eyes. "As a matter of fact, they are. But their new puppy is not named Scout, and

18

it's not a German shepherd. They got tired of waiting, so they adopted a mixed-breed puppy from the shelter. They brought Scamp home yesterday."

"Oh, dear," said Mrs Peterson.

"That's good, though," Lizzie said. "Those dogs at the shelter need homes, too." She knew that because she volunteered one day a week at the local animal shelter, Caring Paws.

"You're absolutely right," said Meg. "Well, let's hope that the *third* family on my list is ready for a pup." She dialled another number and stood listening as the phone rang and rang. "Nobody's home," she said. "But there's a message on their answering machine." She held up a finger as she listened. Then she hung up, sighing. "They're away on holiday – for a whole month!" Meg shook her head. "I don't believe this."

For a moment, they all just stood and watched the dogs play in the yard. "I wish I could take

Scout myself," Meg said. "She is *such* a little cutie. And smart, too. I bet you could train that dog to do anything."

"So, why don't you adopt her?" Lizzie thought Meg would be the *perfect* person for Scout.

"I'd love to, but I can't." Meg shook her head sadly. "Casey and I have to travel all over the place at a moment's notice. That's how it is when you're a search-and-rescue team. So there's no way I can be responsible for a puppy."

"So what are you going to do with Scout?" Jack asked.

Lizzie noticed that he had a certain gleam in his eye. That meant he was thinking the same thing she was. Avoiding her mum's eyes, she asked Meg, "Won't Scout need a foster home?"

"She sure will," Meg said. "I'd love to find her a permanent home with someone who could train her for search and rescue, but that could take some time. Meanwhile, she'll need a loving temporary home."

Lizzie and Jack turned to Mum at the same time. "Mum?" Lizzie asked. They knew she was the one who would need convincing. Dad loved dogs – the more the merrier. "Please?" This time, Jack and Lizzie spoke at the same time.

Mum was looking at the dogs. Casey had curled up for a nap, and both puppies had flopped down beside her. Scout was tucked into the curve of Casey's belly, and Buddy had his chin resting on Scout's leg. All three dogs looked peaceful and happy.

"Well," Mum said, "it does seem as if Buddy enjoys having a friend. Maybe Scout would help him burn off some energy."

"Yesss!" Jack threw a fist into the air.

"All *right*!" yelled Lizzie.

"Yay!" The Bean squealed with delight. He probably didn't even know what was making Jack and Lizzie so happy, but he knew it was time to celebrate.

21

Lizzie turned to Meg. "We'll help you find Scout a forever home," she promised.

"Hold on there." Mum put her hands on her hips. "I haven't said yes yet."

But Lizzie and Jack and the Bean didn't even hear her. They had run down into the yard to tell Scout the good news. She was going to be their foster puppy!

Chapter Four

"Look! Meg and Casey are already here!" Jack pointed to the bright blue van in the school car park. It was Friday morning, and he and Lizzie had just arrived at school.

"Cool!" Lizzie said. "I can't wait to see Casey in action."

"I wonder if the policeman is coming, too," said Sammy, Jack's best friend. The three of them – Lizzie, Jack, and Sammy – had walked to school together, the way they always did.

"He is," said someone behind them. Lizzie turned to see Daphne Drake, the most popular girl in fourth year. "Know how I know?" she asked. "'Cause Officer Frost is my uncle, that's how."

Officer Frost. That must be the policeman friend

Meg had talked about. Lizzie saw Jack and Sammy rolling their eyes at each other. She knew what that meant. They thought Daphne was a show-off.

Lizzie agreed. But she couldn't help showing off a little, too. "Really?" she asked. "I guess he knows our friend Meg, then. She has a really great search-and-rescue dog named Casey. And we're fostering a puppy for her. Scout. That's the puppy's name."

Daphne shrugged. "Is Meg a police officer?" she asked.

"Well, no," said Lizzie. "She's a firefighter."

"My uncle James has five medals," Daphne boasted. "For brave stuff he did. And his dog, Thor, has two."

Lizzie could top that. "Meg's dog, Casey, was named the dog hero of the year last year!" she said. Lizzie had seen Casey's certificate down at the fire station.

"Hmph," was all Daphne had to say to that.

Lizzie saw her best friend, Maria, getting off

the bus. "Gotta go! See you," Lizzie said to Jack, Sammy, and Daphne. Then she ran over to talk to Maria.

"Hey, how's Scout?" Maria asked. She loved dogs nearly as much as Lizzie did. And she knew all about dogs that helped people. Maria's mother, who was blind, had a guide dog – a beautiful yellow Labrador retriever named Simba.

"Scout is *awesome*," Lizzie reported. "She and Buddy do nothing but play, play, play all day long. If they're not playing, they're sleeping. Or eating, of course." She laughed. "I think Scout has grown about two inches in just the last few days. She's going to be a huge dog."

"As big as Casey?" Maria had met Casey once when she and Lizzie were down at the fire station.

"Bigger," Lizzie said. "She'll be a great search-and-rescue dog if we can get her the right home."

Just then, the bell rang and everybody headed inside.

Lizzie and Maria's teacher, Mrs Abeson, was

standing at the door of their classroom. "Don't take off your coats, class," she said. "We have an outdoor assembly first thing today."

Everybody started talking at once. Mrs Abeson folded her arms and waited patiently for silence. "We're going to be meeting two very special dogs and their owners this morning," she said. "I want you all to be on your best behavior."

Lizzie raised her hand. "Mrs Abeson?" she asked. "I know one of the dogs, Casey. She belongs to my dad's friend Meg. Remember? The one who rescued Scout?"

Mrs Abeson nodded. She and the class had heard a lot about Scout during the class's morning meetings that week. "That's great, Lizzie. I'm sure Meg is happy to be coming to your school."

As soon as she finished taking the register, Mrs Abeson led Lizzie's class out onto the playground, which was already full of kids. The other fourth-year class and their teacher, Mr Gabi, were there, plus all the second, third, and fifth years and *their*

teachers. Lizzie had heard that the kindergartners and first years weren't invited, since they were kind of young and might be scared of the dogs.

Lizzie saw Jack over by the swing set with Sammy. She waved. He pointed towards the playing field. There was Meg, holding Casey on a leash. Casey was watching all the kids with interest, grinning at the crowd. Lizzie waved at Meg, but she wasn't sure if Meg saw her.

Next to Meg was a man in a police uniform. He looked very serious. He was holding the leash of another German shepherd. His *dog* looked serious, too.

There was a lot of noise on the playground, since everybody was excited about this special assembly. They'd never had an assembly on the playground before, as far as Lizzie could remember. But everybody finally quieted down when the head teacher, Mr Schaeffer, walked out in front of the crowd and whistled.

Mr Schaeffer had a special way of whistling where he stuck two fingers in his mouth. It was *loud*. Lizzie's dad had tried to teach her how to do it, but so far she hadn't got the trick of it.

"We have two – I mean, *four* – very special guests today." Mr Schaeffer looked excited. "I want to welcome Officer Frost and his dog, Thor, and Meg Parker and her dog, Casey. They're going to tell – and show – you a little about how they work with their dogs. Please give them your full attention." He turned to Meg. "Would you like to begin, Meg?"

"Sure!" Meg smiled – right at Lizzie! Then she asked, "How many of you have dogs?"

Lots of kids raised their hands.

"Great! I had a dog when I was your age, too. His name was Joey and we went everywhere together. He was a German shepherd, too. Just like Casey." She leaned down and gave Casey a pat, and Casey wagged her tail. "Joey was a great pet, but Casey is more than just my pet. She's my partner. We work together to help people in trouble."

Meg reached into a duffel bag by her side and pulled out a bright orange vest. "Casey wears this when she is on the job," she explained.

Lizzie noticed that Casey sat up a little straighter when she saw the vest. Her ears perked up, and her eyes brightened.

Meg noticed, too. "Casey *loves* her work," she explained. "She always gets excited when I put her vest on. I'm going to do it now, because we're going to have a little demonstration. I'm going to ask my good friends Lizzie and Jack Peterson to help me out."

Maria thumped Lizzie on the shoulder. "You're famous!"

Lizzie grinned at her friend. Then she and Jack ran to where Meg and Casey were standing.

Chapter Five

"Before we start, let's talk a little about how to act around dogs. Does anyone know the first rule about patting a dog you haven't met before?" Meg asked.

Lizzie's hand shot up. "Ask the owner first," she said. "Some dogs don't like strangers."

"Good," Meg said, nodding. "Also, most dogs don't really like to be hugged by someone they don't know. So, if the owner says it's OK, you can start off by letting the dog sniff your hand. If the dog doesn't shy away, you can pat it gently."

By now, Casey was pushing her head against Lizzie's hand, begging for a pat. Lizzie and Jack scratched between Casey's ears while Meg began to explain how Casey worked.

"Dogs have an excellent sense of smell," Meg said. "In fact, it's about ten thousand times better than ours! So a dog can smell a person even when they're hidden or lost. If I ask Casey to find someone, she'll start sniffing the air, trying to work out where the person is. Then she'll start to run, following the person's smell. When she finds them, she'll run right back to me and bark to let me know. Then she'll lead me to the person."

Meg turned to Lizzie. "I'm going to keep Casey from watching while you go hide behind that tree near the climbing frame, OK? Then Casey gets to play her favourite game, hide-and-seek. She *loves* to be 'it'. I'll ask her to find you. All you have to do is stay still until she brings me back to you."

"Got it," Lizzie said. While Meg distracted Casey, Lizzie ran over to the tree and tucked herself behind it. After a moment, she heard Meg say, "Find Lizzie!"

In about two seconds, Casey was nosing at Lizzie's hand again. Lizzie couldn't help giggling.

"Good girl," she whispered to Casey. Then Casey was off again, heading back to Meg. She barked excitedly to tell Meg she had found the lost person. In another minute, Meg and Casey had appeared at Lizzie's side.

Meg gave Casey a dog biscuit and lots of pats while all the kids and teachers applauded. "Of course," Meg told the excited crowd, "Casey's jobs are usually a lot more complicated. Last month we searched the woods for seven hours before we found a little boy who was lost."

After that, Meg showed some methods she had used to train Casey, starting with a game called "puppy runaways". She had Jack pat Casey, then take off running towards the swing set. Casey bounded right after him, not letting him out of her sight. When she caught up, Jack gave her a biscuit. "That was how I taught Casey that it was a good thing to follow somebody," Meg explained. "We started with a real person, and after a while she started to learn how to follow a person's *smell*, too – the way she did with Lizzie."

Meg smiled at Lizzie and Jack. "Thanks for your help," she said. Lizzie gave Casey one more pat before she and Jack headed back to their class groups.

"I have a great idea," Lizzie whispered to Maria when she was standing next to her friend again.

But before Lizzie could say more, Meg turned to Officer Frost. "Your turn!"

"OK," said the policeman. "Hi, everybody!" He looked down at Thor, who was sitting alertly at his side. "Thor, can you wave hello?" Thor picked up his right front paw and waved. Everybody cheered.

"I wanted to add something to what Meg said about meeting dogs you don't know," said Officer Frost. "Another thing to remember is that some dogs don't like it if you look right into their eyes. They think you are challenging them to fight with you, since that's one way that dogs challenge each other." He asked Meg to demonstrate by looking right at Thor's eyes.

Thor started to growl and bark! Lizzie suddenly understood why some people might be afraid of German shepherds – or of any big dog. But Officer Frost held Thor's leash tightly. As soon as Meg stepped back and looked away, Thor stopped barking.

"Thor is my partner," said Officer Frost. "Just like a human partner, he keeps me company, helps me prevent and solve crimes, and protects me if I'm in trouble."

Lizzie could just imagine how Thor would act if someone tried to hurt Officer Frost! Yikes.

Officer Frost told a story about how Thor had caught a criminal who was running away after robbing a shop. Then he talked some more about how Thor rode around with him in his patrol car all day, and what a typical day was like for the two partners. "He's my best friend," said Officer

Frost, reaching down to pet Thor. "And Thor has some very good friends right here in the community. Don't you, Thor? A class at the high school sponsors him. They spoil Thor rotten with treats and toys."

When Lizzie heard that, her eyes lit up. Maria smiled. Lizzie knew her best friend could already tell what she was thinking. Lizzie was getting *another* great idea!

Chapter Six

"Come on, Scout! Come on, Buddy! Chase me!" Lizzie ran to the end of the garden, looking over her shoulder to see if the puppies were behind her. Sure enough, Scout was bounding along, right on Lizzie's heels! Buddy ambled a little further behind, stopping now and then to sniff the ground or pick up a stick in his mouth.

As soon as school was over, Lizzie and Maria had headed to Lizzie's house. They could hardly wait to see if Scout had what it took to become a search-and-rescue dog some day. That was the first great idea Lizzie had come up with that day during the assembly. Now that they knew how Casey had been trained, they could try it themselves.

Lizzie and Maria had decided to start with puppy runaways, the training game Meg had talked about. Meg had explained that a good search-and-rescue dog really enjoys following and finding people. "They think it's fun," she had said.

Scout definitely seemed to feel that way. She dashed after Lizzie. She followed Maria when Maria ran the other way. And when Sammy and Jack and the Bean came outside, she followed them, too. She followed whoever was running – from end to end of the garden, up onto the deck, back down and around the side of the house, back up on to the deck, and out to the end of the yard again.

Scout thought this was the best game ever! It was so much fun to follow people. Nobody could get away from her! Scout loved the way the children laughed and patted her and kissed her when she ran after them.

Buddy liked the game, too, but not as much as Scout did. He seemed just as happy to chase his own tail as to chase one of the kids.

After they'd run around for a while, Lizzie flopped down on the deck to catch her breath. The others joined her. Scout climbed up in her lap, and Buddy curled up next to Jack.

"Well, I think Scout really has aptitude," Lizzie announced. She rubbed Scout's fuzzy, floppy ears and kissed the top of her head.

"Ap-*what*?" Jack asked.

"Aptitude," Lizzie said again. "It means she has some natural talents that show she could be a good search-and-rescue dog."

"What about Buddy?" Jack asked. He picked up Buddy's paw and waved it in the air. "I want to be a search-and-rescue dog, too!" Jack said, in a squeaky voice that was supposed to be Buddy's.

Lizzie reached over to pet Buddy. "Maybe someday," she said. "But I think you're best just as our sweet Buddy-boy."

"If you ask me, police dogs are cooler," Sammy said. "I thought Thor was awesome. Did you see the teeth on that dog? I bet the bad guys are really scared of him!"

Lizzie shrugged. "I think Casey's job is more fun," she said. "Thor spends his whole day in the police car, but Casey gets to go all over the country when somebody needs her help."

"True," Maria agreed. "She's a real hero."

"That's why I want our class to sponsor her! She can be *our* class mascot," Lizzie said. "That was my *other* great idea."

"You mean, the way that class at the high school sponsors Thor?" Maria asked.

"Exactly!" said Lizzie. "And when Scout grows up and becomes a search-and-rescue dog, maybe our class can sponsor her, too!" She put Scout down and jumped to her feet. "I have it all worked out," she said, pacing up and down the deck. Scout followed behind her, padding along on her too-big puppy feet.

"We can write emails to Casey, so it'll be like a language arts project. Mrs Abeson will love that. And instead of just buying her treats and toys, like that class does for Thor, we'll raise money to buy Casey things she really *needs*, like, I don't know, maybe booties for her paws. Plus, we can get advice from Meg and Casey on how to train Scout." Lizzie stopped for a breath.

"Maybe we can have a cake sale at school," said Maria, getting into the idea. "That's a great way to raise money."

Lizzie and Maria talked about their idea for the rest of the weekend as they played with the puppies. And at morning meeting on Monday, they had no trouble convincing the rest of the class to sponsor Casey. Lizzie had got Meg's email address from her dad, and she and Maria wrote a note during break that very day. The note really went to Meg, but it was fun to pretend to write to Casey.

To: Casey
From: Mrs Abeson's class
Re: Sponsoring you!
Dear Casey,

Thank you for visiting our school last week. We think you are the greatest! We would like you to be our class mascot and help us with Scout's training. Will you send us a picture of yourself? Also, tell us if there is anything you need, and we will raise the money to get it for you.

Your friends,
Mrs Abeson's class

They heard back the very same day!

To: Mrs Abeson's class
From: Casey
Re: Wow!
Dear Class,

I would be honoured to be your mascot and happy to help with Scout's training. Attached is a picture of me in my vest. I hope you like it! If you really want to get me something I need, maybe you could buy me a flotation vest for water rescues. Lots of my SAR (search-and-rescue) friends have them, and they are really cool. Thanks a million!

Love and barks from your mascot,
Casey

Chapter Seven

During break the next day, Lizzie and Maria made posters for the cake sale. At lunch time, they went around sticking them up. By the end of the day, every kid in school knew that Mrs Abeson's class had a new mascot.

Lizzie was putting up a poster near the nurse's office when Daphne's class passed on their way to the library. "Copycats," Daphne said. "You got that idea from my uncle."

Lizzie just shrugged.

"So what if Daphne thinks we copied?" she asked Maria later that afternoon. They were in the kitchen at Lizzie's house, getting ready to make chocolate chip cookies for the cake sale.

Lizzie rummaged around in a cabinet and pulled out a bag of flour and a box of sugar. Last year her mum had taught Jack and Lizzie her secret cookie recipe, and Lizzie had permission to bake all by herself. Jack was allowed to mix dough, but he was still too young to turn on the oven if Mum wasn't around. "Who cares what Daphne Drake thinks?"

"I definitely don't. Scout!" said Maria, laughing as she pulled the puppy out of the cabinet where the baking sheets were stored. "She's so curious. She just wants to learn about *everything*."

Scout wriggled in Maria's arms. She was curious. Of course she was! It was a big world, and she was only a little puppy. But that wasn't going to keep her from exploring.

Meanwhile, Buddy was chasing a crumpled-up piece of paper around the kitchen. He would bat it away, then run after it, tumbling over his own paws. Finally, he grabbed the piece of paper in his mouth and shook it – so hard that he fell over. He rolled onto his back and chewed on his prize until Lizzie took it away and threw it in the rubbish bin.

"No eating paper, Buddy!" Lizzie said patiently. These days, Buddy seemed to want to taste everything he came across. Maybe it was because he had lost some baby teeth and his adult teeth were coming in.

Buddy looked up at Lizzie. He knew she wasn't really mad at him – but he also knew she wasn't going to give him back the paper. He scrambled to his feet and ran off to find something else to chew on.

"OK, I think we have all the ingredients. Let's check the recipe and make sure." Lizzie looked over the things they had laid out on the kitchen counter: flour, sugar, eggs, butter, vanilla extract, chocolate chips, baking sheets, a mixing bowl, measuring cups and spoons.

"Where is the recipe?" Maria asked.

Lizzie looked around for the handwritten sheet her mother had left out. It was nowhere to be seen. Then she remembered the paper Buddy had been playing with. "Buddy!" she said. "Was that our recipe?"

Buddy looked up at her with a guilty expression on his face. His tail wagged uncertainly. He plopped down on his pudgy behind and held up one paw.

Lizzie sounded mad. Had he done something wrong?

She went back to the rubbish bin and pulled out the crumpled, chewed-up piece of paper. She smoothed it out. Sure enough, it was the cookie recipe. "You silly!" Lizzie shook a finger at Buddy, but she was laughing. Baking cookies was fun. Baking cookies with two puppies in the house was even *more* fun.

Yay! Buddy knew everything was OK now. Lizzie was laughing again.

Lizzie read the recipe over. "I think the only thing we forgot is baking soda." She went over to the cabinet to find some. Scout jumped up to follow her. "Baking powder – no, that's not it," Lizzie muttered as she checked the labels. "Here it is!" She pulled out a small yellow box.

Maria had been checking the recipe. "What about extra butter for greasing the pan?" she asked.

Buddy was busy with something under the table, but now his head popped up. Had he heard his name?

"I said *butter*," Maria said, laughing. "Not Buddy."

Buddy went back to whatever it was he was playing with. Lizzie got some more butter out of the fridge, and the girls began to measure ingredients.

"OK, last thing we add is the chips." Lizzie shook out her arm. Stirring the stiff batter was hard work. "Where are they?" She looked over the counter, which was now a big mess. Used measuring cups, dabs of butter, and spilled flour and sugar were all in a jumble.

Maria looked, too. "I don't see them."

Just then, Scout began to bark. She ran under the table and pulled something away from Buddy. It was the bag of chocolate chips!

"Oh, no!" Lizzie said. "Chocolate can make dogs really, really ill!" She reached down and gently took the package out of Scout's mouth. "Phew," Lizzie said after she'd taken a good look. "He didn't get it open yet. It's just a little slobbered-on."

Maria gave Scout a big hug. "You're already a search-and-rescue dog! You found the chips and stopped Buddy from eating them."

Scout knew she had done something very, very good. She licked Maria's face all over, paying special attention to the spots that were smeared with cookie batter.

When they finished baking the cookies, Lizzie and Maria went upstairs. While Lizzie checked her email, Maria lounged on Lizzie's bed. Both puppies sprawled across her lap. Scout was gnawing gently on Buddy's ear while Buddy tried to eat the belt loops on Maria's jeans.

"I can't wait to give Casey her flotation vest," said Maria.

"Well, you're going to have to." Lizzie was suddenly serious. "Check out this email Meg just sent our class."

To: Mrs Abeson's class
From: Casey
Subject: Off on an adventure
Dear Class,
Just wanted to let you know that Meg and I are off to Mexico. There was a big earthquake there and we are going to help find people who might have got hurt or lost. I can't wait to get to work! I'll keep you posted on all our adventures. Keep up the good work with Scout's training!
Love and barks,
Casey

Chapter Eight

"I'll take three brownies and one of those flap-jacks," said Mr Schaeffer.

Lizzie handed them over with a big smile. "Thanks!" she said as she took the two dollars he gave her. "Casey appreciates your support!"

As the head teacher walked away, Lizzie looked over the table that had started out covered with cookies and cakes. It was already half empty. "Wow, we've sold so much, and it's only eleven-thirty!" Lizzie said to Maria. The two had just arrived to take the last shift of the class bake sale.

"I know," Maria said. "I think it's the pictures that get to everybody." She turned to look at the pictures on the wall behind them. One was a big blowup of the picture Meg had sent. Casey looked like a real hero, standing at attention in her orange vest. There were also some smaller pictures that the girls had taken of Scout practising her puppy runaways.

On either side of the pictures were blowups of Casey's emails. And Maria had drawn a map of Mexico, with a star showing the place where the earthquake had happened. Over the whole display was a big banner that said: HELP MRS ABESON'S CLASS SUPPORT CASEY!

Lizzie looked at the map and felt a twinge in her tummy. Casey and Meg were so far away! And the work they were doing could be dangerous. Whole buildings had been wrecked in the earthquake. Casey was helping to find people who had been trapped inside.

There had only been one email that day, a short one to say that Meg and Casey had arrived in Mexico and that they might not be able to write again for a few days. Lizzie knew she would worry about them until they were both home, safe and sound. Someday Scout might be doing that kind of work, too!

Lizzie picked up another chocolate chip cookie and tossed a coin into the change box. "Split this with me?" She offered a piece to Maria.

Maria took a bite of her half. "These turned out pretty well," she said. "Maybe having two puppies around only adds to the recipe."

Lizzie laughed. "Yeah. Good thing we noticed Buddy licking the baking sheets after I greased them. They definitely needed washing before we used them. That puppy gets into everything!"

"Kathy can't wait to see him and meet Scout today," Maria said.

Kathy was Maria's riding teacher. She and her husband ran a stable nearby, and they had adopted Rascal, a Jack Russell terrier puppy the Petersons had fostered.

Kathy had invited Lizzie and Jack to bring the two puppies over to play while Maria had her lesson that afternoon. Kathy and her husband had fenced off a huge area for Rascal to play in, so the puppies would really be able to run – without being able to run away! Kathy called it Rascal's playpen.

By the time the last of the lunch crowd had disappeared, Maria and Lizzie were left with a nearly empty table. They counted up the money they'd made.

"I have thirty-three dollars," Lizzie announced.

"Plus fifteen seventy-six," added Maria, adding up the piles of coins she'd stacked. "I don't know who gave us that penny."

"Every cent helps!" said Lizzie. She was adding up the total. "Forty-eight seventy-six!" she announced. "Wow, almost fifty dollars. We can get the flotation vest for Casey – and maybe we can also get a little orange vest for Scout. That way she can start to feel like a real search-and-rescue dog."

"Maybe my dad can drive us to the pet shop on the way home today," Maria said. "I know

Casey and Meg won't be back for a while, but it would be nice to have presents ready to welcome them home."

After school Maria's father picked up Maria, Lizzie, Jack, Scout, and Buddy and drove them to the stable.

"Oh, look at this little girl!" Kathy said when they all climbed out of the car. She knelt down to say hello to Scout. Buddy ran over, too, jumping into her arms and licking her face. Kathy laughed. "Yes, hello to you, too," she said to Buddy.

"Where's Rascal?" Lizzie asked.

"He's inside," Kathy told her. "I thought *three* puppies might be a bit too much." She was stroking Scout. "What a sweet girl," she said. "Have you found a home for her yet?"

Jack shook his head. "Not so far," he said. He and Lizzie had made some posters and they had put them up around town, but the Petersons had only got one phone call, from somebody who really wanted an older dog. Jack and Lizzie didn't mind. They wanted to make sure Scout found a great home, hopefully with someone who wanted to keep training her for search and rescue. Meg had promised to help when she got back from Mexico. In the meantime, it was great for Buddy to have a friend.

"Well," said Kathy, getting up and dusting off her knees, "I could play with these two all day. But Maria has a lesson. Why don't I show you Rascal's playpen? After we finish riding, we'll join you in there for some more playtime. Maybe I'll bring Rascal then, too." She led them behind the barn to a fenced-in area.

Lizzie couldn't believe how big Rascal's playpen was. It was like a park, with trees, bushes, and even a stream to splash in.

"This is great!" Lizzie said. "A safe new place for you two to play." She bent down and unclipped the puppies' leashes.

Buddy dashed off immediately, with Scout tearing after him. They zoomed around, stopping every few seconds to sniff all the new, exciting smells.

Hey, check this out! Over here! Whee! Buddy had *found a mud puddle to roll in.*

"Oh, Buddy!" Lizzie said. "What a mess."

Scout was busy sniffing a trail she had found. Another dog used this place! Scout followed his scent from bush to bush.

"Scout!" called Jack. "Don't wander off too far!"

"Let's play a game with them," Lizzie suggested. "How about puppy runaways? That's great training for Scout."

"No, let's play hide-and-seek!" Jack said. "Like Meg did with me at the demonstration.

I'll go hide behind that tree, and you send Scout and Buddy to find me."

When Jack was hidden, Lizzie called the puppies. Scout came running, but Buddy was still busy sniffing around. "Oh, well," said Lizzie. "Scout's the one we really want to train. Go find Jack, Scout! Find him!"

Scout looked up at the girl. She wanted something. What was it?

"Here, I'll show you," said Lizzie. "Let's find him together!" She ran, leading Scout closer to where Jack was hiding. "Find him!" she said again, hoping to teach Scout what that meant.

Scout sniffed. She smelled the very special, wonderful scent of someone she loved. Jack! She bounced around the tree. There he was! She jumped up happily, barking. How wonderful to

find her boy! And now he was giving her some treats. Yum!

"I think she gets the idea," said Lizzie. "She is a fast learner. Let's try again. I'll distract her while you hide." Lizzie looked around for Buddy and spotted him over by some big boulders. He looked happy to be exploring on his own. He didn't seem interested in hide-and-seek, but that was OK.

Jack ran off again and hid himself behind a bush. After a minute, Lizzie told Scout to "find him!" Scout took off like a rocket – straight for the bush.

Hide-and-seek with Scout was so much fun. Jack hid again, then Lizzie hid twice. Scout got better and better at finding them quickly. It was hard to fool her! She could sniff them out no matter how well they hid. Her nose was amazing.

Finally, when both Jack and Lizzie had run, out of puppy treats, they plopped down on the ground for a rest. Scout put her head on Jack's knee and stretched out one paw on to Lizzie's leg. Lizzie scratched the puppy's ears. "Great job, Scout," she said. "Maybe you can teach Buddy how to do it, too."

"Where is Buddy?" Jack asked. "Buddy!" he called.

Lizzie expected Buddy to come galloping over. But he didn't. She started calling, too. "Buddy! Where are you?"

"Maybe he thinks he's playing hide-and-seek," said Jack.

Lizzie called again. She knew Buddy had to be somewhere nearby. After all, the whole area was fenced in. But suddenly, she was beginning to worry. How could she have let him wander off? She felt terrible. She had got so wrapped up in training Scout that she had forgotten – just for a moment – about the most important little puppy in the world: *her* puppy, Buddy!

Chapter Nine

"Buddy!" Lizzie called.

"Buddy! Come!" Jack shouted.

Lizzie tried to do that fingers-in-the-mouth whistle, but as usual it didn't work. So she clapped her hands instead. "Buddy!" she yelled again.

Buddy did not appear.

"We'd better start looking for him," said Lizzie. "What if there's a hole in the fence or something?" She started off toward the place where she'd seen Buddy last, near the boulders. Jack and Scout followed her.

Buddy wasn't near the boulders.

Buddy wasn't behind a tree.

Buddy wasn't trapped in some bushes.

Buddy was nowhere to be found!

Lizzie turned to Jack. "Maybe you should go get Kathy," she said. "I'll keep looking."

Jack nodded, looking serious. "We'll find him, right?" he asked.

Lizzie gave her brother a hug. She knew how worried he was. Buddy was the puppy they had wanted for so many years! They both loved him so much. "He'll be fine," she said. "I'm sure he just found something that seems more interesting than us right now. He's probably sniffing so loudly he can't even hear us calling him."

Jack nodded again. Then he took off toward the gate to get Kathy.

Lizzie looked around. How could Buddy have disappeared so quickly? It had only been a few minutes since she had last seen him. She decided to walk around the length of the whole fence, calling for him along the way. "Come on, Scout," she said. "Let's find Buddy."

Scout's ears pricked up when she heard that word. She knew what "find" meant! This game was the most fun ever. But why didn't Lizzie sound happy, the way she usually did when they played? Scout glanced up at Lizzie with a worried look. Then she put her nose in the air and started sniffing for her friend Buddy.

"Buddy! Buddy!" Lizzie called as she walked along the fence. She didn't see any holes or gaps that her little puppy could have climbed through. As she walked, she also looked toward the centre of the playpen. She was hoping to see the quick flick of a tail or a flash of the white heart on Buddy's chest. But there was no sign of Buddy.

Scout trotted along in front of Lizzie, sniffing at everything. She was wagging her tail, and her ears were as close to pointed as Lizzie had ever seen them. "You're a good girl, Scout," said Lizzie. "I know you'll help find Buddy."

There was that word again. Scout sniffed even harder.

Suddenly, Lizzie gasped. As she rounded a corner, she saw that a tall tree beside the stream had fallen over, crushing the fence beneath it. Scout ran over to the place where the fence had broken, sniffing like mad. "Oh, no!" Lizzie said. Instantly, she knew that Buddy must have escaped from the playpen. Now he could be *anywhere*! They had to find him quickly, before he could get into trouble.

Lizzie looked behind her, hoping to see Kathy and the others arriving. But there was nobody in sight. She knew what she had to do. "Come here, Scout!" she said. She clipped a lead onto Scout's collar, so Scout couldn't run away, too. Then she gave the command. "Let's go! Find him! Find Buddy!"

Scout and Lizzie scrambled over the fallen tree

and the broken fence. They splashed through the little stream, which continued on the other side of the fence. "Look!" Lizzie said. There were paw prints in the mud. "Buddy must have gone this way!"

Scout seemed to understand. She leaned into the lead, pulling Lizzie along the path of the stream. They followed the footprints a long way, as the stream wound this way and that.

Soon, Lizzie began to hear the sound of cars. Her heart started thumping hard. There must be a road nearby! "Buddy!" she called. Her mouth was so dry that she hardly made any sound. She licked her lips. "Buddy!" she called again.

Then, suddenly, Scout began to pull even harder on the leash. She dragged Lizzie all the way to the edge of a road where cars were whizzing by. "Oh, no," Lizzie said. If Buddy had tried to cross the road . . . she couldn't even think about what might have happened.

But at the last minute, Scout did not climb up onto the road. Instead, she headed straight for a big pipe that went *under* the road. She poked her head inside and barked.

And Buddy barked back.

To: Casey
From: Lizzie
Subject: Scout's a hero!
Dear Casey,
You would be so proud of little Scout! Today she found Buddy, who was stuck in a culvert, one of those pipes that water goes through. Then she rescued him, since the pipe was too small for any people to crawl into. We were so happy to see him! Buddy was happy, too. He licked everybody in sight. Then he licked us all again. Maybe he'll stay out of trouble for a little while this time!

I hope you're doing well in Mexico. Our class

can't wait to see you again! When will you be back?

Love,

Lizzie

To: Lizzie

From: Casey

Subject: Coming home

Dear Lizzie,

Wow! That Scout is something else. Sounds like all your training is really paying off! Thanks for the news about her and Buddy's adventure.

I will be seeing all of you in person sooner than I thought. I had a little adventure of my own down here in Mexico, and Meg is bringing me home early. We'll tell you all about it when we get there.

Love and barks,

Casey

Chapter Ten

Casey had written to Mrs Abeson's class, too. All day the next day Mrs Abeson had to keep asking the class to settle down. Everyone was buzzing with excitement about when Casey would get home from Mexico. Plus, Lizzie had shared the story about Scout finding and rescuing Buddy. The class was proud of Scout, too. They couldn't wait until she was a real search-and-rescue dog, so they could sponsor her.

But Lizzie knew that what Scout really needed was a for ever family to live with. She was such an amazing puppy! She needed a home with people who would really appreciate how clever she was and what she could do. Lizzie was really hoping that Meg would be able to help find Scout a perfect home with one of her search-and-rescue friends.

Lizzie and Jack were walking home from school that afternoon when their dad pulled up next to them in the family van. "Hop in!" he said. "Meg just called from the airport. She and Casey have just arrived. We're going to pick them up!"

"Really?" Lizzie could hardly believe it. She and Jack climbed into the van. Lizzie watched the scenery go by, thinking about the last time she had come this way, when she and Meg had picked up Scout. That hadn't been so very long ago – but Lizzie already felt as if she had known Scout for ever.

It wasn't going to be easy to say goodbye to Scout when the time came for her to go to her fo ever home. That was the hard part about fostering puppies. Lizzie and Jack were always sad to let them go. But every puppy was so special. Lizzie felt very lucky to be able to spend even a little time with each one.

Soon Dad pulled into the airport car park. He, Lizzie, and Jack got out and headed across the walkway into the small terminal. Lizzie looked around. The building was full of people walking up and down, looking for their baggage, and getting in line for tickets. But where was Meg? Where was Casey?

Then she saw a woman bending over a dog's travel crate, opening the door. A brown-and-black head poked out. Pointy nose, big pointy ears – it was Casey! Lizzie started running.

Meg stood up and turned to give Lizzie a hug. Her face was serious. "Lizzie—" she began.

But Lizzie had already bent down to say hello to Casey. Why wasn't she coming out of her crate? Lizzie patted Casey's head and scratched her between her ears, the way she liked. "Hey, girl," she said. Then she saw the bandages. Casey's shoulder was wrapped in gauze.

By then, Jack and Dad had caught up. "What is

it?" Dad asked Lizzie. He could tell she was upset.

"Casey's hurt," Lizzie said. She looked at Meg. "What is it? What happened?"

"Remember when Casey was limping that time at your house?" Meg asked. "Well, she fell when she was climbing into a cellar in Mexico to save a little girl, and that old shoulder injury got a lot worse. She had to have an operation."

Dad put an arm around Meg's shoulders. "I'm sorry," he said.

Meg nodded. "So am I. But she's not in pain any more. The vet said she'll heal quickly and be able to walk around again really soon."

"That's good," Lizzie said. She and Jack were kneeling by Casey's crate, patting her gentle face. "So when will she be able to go back to work?"

Meg didn't answer.

Lizzie looked up to see that Meg's eyes were filled with tears. She was shaking her head. "Never," she said. "Casey is going to have to retire from search-and-rescue work. I'm losing my partner."

"Wow." Lizzie didn't know what to say. That was terrible news! Casey was so good at what she did. "But she'll still be your pet, right?" she asked.

"Of course!" said Meg. "This girl is going to have the cushiest retirement ever. I'm going to get her a big soft bed, and feed her sweets every day, and rent DVDs for her to watch." Lizzie could tell Meg was trying to sound happy, but the tears were still in her eyes.

"I'll come over and take her for walks," Lizzie promised. "And she can still be our class mascot!" She knew it wasn't much, but she wanted to say something to make Meg feel better.

On the way home, Meg told them about the things Casey had done in Mexico. "She was amazing," Meg said. "She found at least five people who were stuck inside buildings. That little girl was the last one, and Casey managed to pull her out of the wreckage, even with her shoulder hurting so terribly."

"She should get a medal," Jack said.

"She's a hero," Meg agreed.

Dad had invited Meg over for dinner, so they drove straight home. Dad helped Meg lift Casey out of the van, and they brought her inside and laid her down gently near the fireplace. Mum had made lasagna and garlic bread, and the house smelled wonderful.

Buddy and Scout galloped over to say hello to Casey. "Easy, you two!" said Lizzie. Jack grabbed Buddy and picked him up.

But Scout went straight to Casey. She seemed to know it was important to be gentle with the big, injured German shepherd. The older dog and Scout touched noses, and Casey's tail thumped on the floor. Then Scout curled right up next to Casey, as if she knew Casey needed comforting. Casey's eyes closed contentedly as she lay her head down and fell asleep.

"Casey's all worn out from the trip," Meg whispered. "Boy, does she love that little pup."

Watching the two dogs together, Lizzie had one more great idea. She crossed her fingers. It was probably too much to hope for – but Meg would be the *perfect* person to adopt Scout. After all, Meg was going to need a new partner. Scout needed a new home. And Casey needed a friend.

Lizzie looked up at Meg. "You know, Casey really wants to teach Scout about being a search-and-rescue dog," she said. "And Scout would love to keep Casey company so she won't get bored since she's not working any more."

"It's funny. . ." Meg's eyes were filled with tears again, but now she was smiling. "I have been thinking the exact same thing."

"Really?" Lizzie grinned at Meg, then reached out to pat Scout. "So, does that mean you're going to adopt Scout?"

"That's right!" Meg gave Scout a kiss on the head. "And I hope you'll help me train her, too!"

"I would love to!" Lizzie was thrilled that she'd get to spend so much time with Scout.

Lizzie looked over at her family. Jack was holding Buddy close, but Buddy still managed to stretch his neck out to lick the Bean's nose. Mum reached out to pat Buddy, and Dad put an arm around Mum.

The Petersons smiled at one another. Once again, they had helped a puppy find the perfect for ever home.

Puppy Tips

Some dogs are more than just loving pets. Dogs that can find lost people or help the police are true heroes. Is there a dog on the police force where you live?

Police dogs and search-and-rescue dogs need a lot of training. Their owners work hard with them – but the dogs make it all worthwhile. And when the dogs retire, they usually live the rest of their lives with their owners, enjoying a relaxing old age!

Dear Reader,

One of the most fun things I ever did was to help rescue some puppies who needed homes. My friend is part of a border collie rescue group. She and I drove to pick up three little border collie puppies and we got to spend the afternoon playing with them and watching them chase one another around. I will never forget how cute they were.

My friend kept one of the puppies and named her Bodi. Now Bodi is a beautiful grown-up dog who is a good friend to my dog, Django.

Yours from the Puppy Place,
Ellen Miles